Anaximancy

Simon Christiansen

Copyright © 2023 Simon Christiansen

All rights reserved.

ISBN: 978-87-94505-02-4

DEDICATION

This story is dedicated to all those readers who write reviews on Amazon, Goodreads, and similar sites.

Your support means the world to us writers.

CONTENTS

Acknowledgments	i
Anaximancy	1
Tenebrous Pilgrimage	29
Polis Cum Laude	30
Blurb	31
About the Author	32

ACKNOWLEDGMENTS

I would like to thank my family, friends, and readers, who gave me invaluable support and feedback during the writing of this story.

I would also like to acknowledge the Greek philosopher Anaximander, whose groovy cosmological system was the inspiration for this story.

The two poems following the story were previously published by poetry journals. I would therefore like to acknowledge:

Neologism Poetry Journal, which published *Polis Cum Laude*, and

Revolver Literary Magazine, the publisher of *Tenebrous Pilgrimage*.

ANAXIMANCY

"We choose to go through the Moon!" The speaker's voice came loud and clear from the sound system, audible over the roar of the engines. Every citizen had to hear the speech, even the crew.

"We choose to go through the Moon and do other things, not because they are easy, but because they are hard. When Columbus sailed over the edge of the top of the cylinder, he taught humanity that there is no "new world" waiting out there; we have only the one, and we must fight to keep it!"

The acceleration pushed Sophia Aetós against the seat. On the viewscreen, the city of Athens stretched out beneath them, towers of steel standing side by side with temples of ancient marble. The city shrunk, turning into a toy model; tiny dots of moving vehicles barely visible, then not visible at all.

"Scientists say the length of the cylinder is one-third the diameter of the habitable top. What was Columbus thinking as he fell, I wonder?"

The metal frame of the ship groaned. Sophia looked at the viewscreen again and gasped. The entire top of the cylinder was visible. The three continents of Europa, Asia, and Libya, separated by the Mediterranean, the Black Sea, and the river Nile, like three slices of a giant pizza. The Edge Ocean surrounded the continents, bounded by the edge of the top. Those foolish enough to doubt this basic fact of geography had followed Columbus down the side.

"The earth rests in space due to the principle of indifference: There is no reason for it to move in any direction rather than any other, so it remains where it has always been."

She idly wondered if there was a different civilization on the opposite base of the cylinder. Answering that question would be the goal of a different expedition. Since early childhood, she had been mesmerized by the Moon. She would be the first to uncover its mysteries.

"We, however, must not be indifferent. We must MOVE, move towards progress and victory. Only through this movement can we secure the future for the children of Europa."

"Hell of a view, eh cap?" Neferu Ana's voice cut through the engine's rumble, the creaking of the metal, and the speaker's voice.

Fighting against the acceleration, Sophia turned her head towards Neferu, who met her gaze with eyes wide with wonder, her sharp nose vibrating with the ship. Her lithe arms grabbed the edges of her seat as if she was afraid to fall, though she was strapped in. As delicate as she was lovely.

"In the past, many believed the Moon to be merely a big rock floating in the sky. The great scientist Anaximander demonstrated its true nature: A massive hole in one of the hollow rings of bark surrounding the earth, through which the primeval fire shines upon us. In this fire, we will forge the future of humanity!"

Minutes of applause followed before the sound system

finally cut off.

The rumble of the engines subsided, turning into a low murmur emerging from the floor and the walls. The creaking of the metal stopped. Sophia exhaled, realizing she had been holding her breath.

She unbuckled herself and slid from the chair, landing on the carpeted floor beneath them. The friction of the carpet kept her standing against the gentle swaying of the ship. She had told the committee that a bare metal floor would be too slippery.

Neferu landed on the floor next to her. Control panels and data machines surrounded them in the circular room. The main viewscreen still showed the cylinder below, quickly receding.

"Gravity feels normal," said Neferu.

"Of course," said Sophia. "The natural place of human beings is on the top of the cylinder. As long as the rocket points upwards, our bodies will try to reach the top and stop at the floor."

Neferu stood perfectly still, transfixed by the image on the viewscreen. "We're the first people to see the entire top," she said.

Sophia glanced at the screen again. "Make sure to get all the details. After all, you're the artist."

They hugged and cheered.

"What are you two turtledoves doing down there?" Sophia looked up to see Valeria Vita peek down from the hatch in the ceiling, slick black hair spilling from her shoulders. "Come and join us!" The ladder unfolded from the hatch, new segments extending from the end until it reached the floor.

On the floor above, four bunks unfolded from the wall, equipped with firm mattresses. Next to each bunk stood a small table with a single drawer for personal items. Valeria stood by one of her tables, inspecting her uniform with a hand mirror. She flicked away a speck of dust, and the uniform was spotless.

Reza Nazari sat on the neighboring bunk, adjusting his prosthetic arm with a screwdriver. The scars on his face made it hard to judge his emotions; his right eye was milky white; the left sky-blue. "Captain," he said and rose from the bunk.

"Good," she said. "We all survived the launch. Reza, will you accompany me to the lab?"

He nodded curtly and pushed a button on the wall. A hatch opened in the ceiling, and a ladder unfolded.

"Valeria, you have the ship while I'm gone."

The lab shone with polished tables and shining beakers. The glass cabinets adorning the wall displayed every scientific instrument known to man. The machines on the tables slept, awaiting material for analysis.

"Everything is in flawless condition, Captain," said Reza. "I cleaned and inspected the place three times before launch."

"And you are confident that the machinery will be up to the task?"

He shrugged. "As confident as any human can be when it concerns the unknown. So far, Apeiron has only been hypothesized by physicists. We will be the first to study an actual sample. If we can find one."

"The gods smile upon us," said Sophia. She pushed another button, and another ladder fell from the ceiling, leading to the final segment of the ship, the one they jokingly referred to as the space attic: A dark room with a conical roof at the end of the vessel, containing the airlock. When she had satisfied herself that everything was in order, she returned to rejoin her crew.

In the control room, Neferu painted. Her easel stood in

front of the viewscreen, and the brush danced across the canvas, on which a birds-eye view of the earth gradually came into focus, seemingly accumulating details all by itself.

"It's beautiful," said Sophia.

Neferu laughed. "Indeed, but that's not the point. The ecclesia wants something humbling, to remind us of how small we are."

***

"Captain," said Valeria. "We're approaching the first star ring."

Sophia looked at the viewscreen. They were now close enough to the stars to see the contours of the ring – a gnarly back-like substance somehow strong enough to contain the endless conflagration inside. Through holes in the surface, white light shone upon the ship and the earth below. Uncountable numbers of such hollow rings surrounded them at different angles, accounting for every star in the sky.

"Do you want me to go through one of the stars, cap?" asked Valeria with a roguish smile.

"Tempting, but let's wait for the moon. Those star holes are a bit too small for my taste, and scientists believe that the fire in the moon ring is cooler."

When they had passed the rings, there were no longer any stars in the sky. Only the moon shone through endless darkness. The sun hid behind the earth.

"No holes on the other side of the star rings," said Reza. "That knowledge alone makes the trip worth it."

"The priests are right," said Neferu. "They are made for us."

"What do you think, Reza? Does this mean there will be no moon on the other side of the moon ring either?"

He shrugged, and his mechanical shoulder whirred. "No point in hypothesizing. If there isn't, we will exit through the same Moon through which we entered."

They retired to sleep in the endless night. They rose to see the moon filling the entire viewscreen, incandescent through the portholes. This close, they could see the billowing flames of the white fire through the enormous hole. The light from the portholes made droplets of sweat run down Sophia's arms.

"You think the ship will hold?" said Sophia.

Reza raised an eyebrow in reply. "If it doesn't, it won't take long."

"Valeria, take us in."

"Aye, captain." The hum of the engine increased; the glass in the portholes dimmed. White fire now filled the entire viewscreen. The whole ship groaned and creaked, and the floor shifted between Sophia's feet. Even through the dimmed portholes, the Moon fire shone.

The ship sighed a final time and then calmed. They were through.

Sophia thought the room felt hotter, but not by much.

"It holds," said Reza in a tone that brooked no argument.

Sophia collapsed into the command chair and wiped her forehead. "Start a continuous scan of our surroundings. We don't want to miss anything."

Neferu had already set up her easel and was busy smearing white paint all over the canvas. In the density and the texture of the pigment, Sophia thought she saw billowing flames.

**

She woke to the sound of the alarm. A dull, repetitive beeping. She jerked upright in bed, and sweat fell into her eyes, covering her vision with blurry prisms. She wiped her eyes and blinked. She licked her lips and tasted salt. *Why am I so hot?* she thought.

Neferu, Valeria, and Reza were awake as well. Reza had jumped straight out of bed and was already nearly into his uniform. The two others were still awakening.

Sophia grabbed for her uniform on her dresser. "What's going on?"

"It shouldn't be this hot," said Reza, now fully dressed. "Something is wrong." He climbed down the ladder with the speed of an athlete.

Sophia met him in the control room, where he was inspecting the wires behind one of the control panels. The panel had been torn off and thrown to the floor, where it still wobbled.

"The cooling system is down," he said without looking in her direction. "We are going to get cooked."

"How is that possible? Everything was fine yesterday!"

"I have my suspicions," he said. "But there is no time."

"Can you fix it?"

"I don't know. The damage is extensive."

Valeria slid down the ladder and dropped into the pilot's chair. "What's the sitch?"

"How fast can you get us back to the hole?" said Sophia.

"We've been moving forward for nearly a full day. Even at maximum thrust, it will be four to five hours, at least."

Reza slammed his bionic arm into the wall, leaving a dent. "We have about an hour before we faint from the heat. The suits will sustain us for maybe another hour. Running is not an option."

"Well, can you fix it in less than two hours?"

Reza looked at the wires and slowly shook his head. "Even

if I manage to fix this, it will be too late. There is only one option: Someone must go outside and access the mechanism through the external hatch."

"Very well, then. We would need to test the suits sooner or later. As captain, it falls to me to lead the way. Valeria, you have the ship."

***

The airlock door in the attic opened with a hiss, and Sophia stepped into the liminal chamber between the dark interior and dazzling surroundings. The darkened glass of the helmet made it hard to see as she moved through the airlock. The door closed behind her, and it was dark and quiet for a moment. Then the outer airlock door opened, and white flames rushed into the metal chamber.

She shut her eyes and held her breath instinctively as the flames filled the room and light burned her face. Even through the darkened, polarized glass, it was like standing in bright sunlight. She felt the heat rise and prayed that the suit would hold.

After a few seconds, she opened her eyes and blinked. Her eyes watered, but the filter glass made the light endurable. Through the roaring flames, she could make out the walls of the airlock and the open doorway at the other end. She walked through the door and into the fires of the Moon.

The suction devices kept her attached to the hull's exterior as she climbed the ship's length. The flames were just cool enough to be manageable by the suit. Not for the first time, she wondered how long it would take before humanity was ready to explore the sun.

Reza's voice crackled in her ear: "You are getting close.

How is the suit holding up?"

"Fine," she replied. "It's like a sauna in here, but nothing I can't handle."

A few minutes later: "You are there. Try to find the access panel labeled 'krúos'."

The filter glass allowed her to read the letters etched onto the panel. "I have it."

"Good. You must drill a hole straight through the center without letting the flames penetrate."

The suit's maintenance drill whirred, a faint tingling in her arm. She felt it go through and kept the arm steady. Drilling too deep could destroy the delicate hydraulics.

The display in her helmet showed her the view of the camera tube, now snaking its way into the hull from the tip of the drill. She felt like she floated through a jumble of wires, tubes, and circuitry board.

"I have the image feed," said Reza. "Here is what you need to do."

She followed instructions, untangling wires, and reestablishing connections, while she felt the heat inside the suit increasing.

"The flow has been reenabled," said Reza. "I should be able to fix the rest from the inside."

Sophia breathed a sigh of relief and retracted the camera tube, sealing the hole in the plate with self-hardening foam. She climbed towards the top of the ship, idly wondering why they couldn't have added airlock doors at both ends.

An alarm on her heads-up display blinked. The heat was increasing fast. How? Why? A leak?

"Something's wrong with your suit," said Reza. "Get back ASAP."

She rolled her eyes. "I wasn't planning on taking a

vacation."

Sweat tickled her eyes and ran down her arms. She wondered if her sweaty hands would lose their grip, cursed herself for being silly, and wondered about her mental state. The air burned her lips when she breathed.

The tip of the ship was impossibly distant and not getting any closer. Was she even climbing in the right direction? She blinked for a few seconds – was it only a few seconds? – and blacked out for an indeterminate moment.

Her destination seemed even farther away than before. She tried to keep climbing, but her hand stuck to the hull; she was too weak to remove it. She looked at the suction cup as if willing it to let go, but it ignored her. She licked her lips and tasted blood in the cracks.

She looked around her as if someone nearby might be able to assist, and then she saw it: Hiding behind the flames, indescribable and unbounded by any concept in her mind, it beckoned. She passed out.

***

Cool water trickled between her lips. The air no longer burned her skin. "I think she is awake," someone said, but the voice sounded fuzzy and far away. She coughed and swallowed the remaining water.

She blinked, and the worried faces of the crew came into focus above her. The bunk felt firm beneath.

"What happened?" she asked and winced. Her lips were so dry that it hurt to talk.

"There was a leak in your suit," said Reza. "Neferu insisted on going out there for you. We would be recovering a charred corpse by now if she hadn't."

"With all due respect," said Valeria. "Isn't it your responsibility to check the suits?"

"I checked everything yesterday. There were no leaks."

"Could you have missed something," asked Neferu.

"No."

Sophia pushed herself upright on the bunk and greedily drank from the canteen that Neferu handed her. The minerals gave the water a salty taste. Her lips burned, and the surroundings wobbled. She grabbed the edge of the bunk and things fell into place.

"What are you suggesting?" she asked Reza.

"Sabotage," he said.

There was an awkward silence as everyone looked at the others.

"I didn't want to kill myself," said Sophia. "So, you say Neferu or Valeria tried to kill me?"

Reza shrugged. "The coolant system failure didn't happen by itself either. Whoever did this was willing to risk their own life. I wouldn't rule you out."

"What about you," said Neferu. "Aren't you the obvious suspect? You are responsible for technical maintenance and equipment. We have only your word that you inspected the suit yesterday."

"True. If I were in your position, I wouldn't rule me out either."

Sophia jumped from the bunk and threw up her arms. "Great. So, we are all potential saboteurs. Spreading that suspicion is itself a former of sabotage. How can we continue the mission if we can't trust each other? This must be the Asians. They wanted to be the first through the moon."

"We need to find the spy," said Valeria, studying each of them with hungry eyes.

"I'm the captain," said Sophia. "Leading this mission has been my life's dream. I have a doctorate in cosmology and have wanted to know what was inside the Moon since I was a child. No reward would convince me to sabotage my mission so someone else could be first."

"I'm an artist," said Neferu. "It's a great privilege to be the first to immortalize the cosmos in my art. I'll be famous for the rest of human history. Why would I give that up?"

"I fought the Asians in a privateer vessel during both wars," said Valeria. "I sunk dozens of their ships but lost most of my friends. I know how devious they can be. I would never trust them."

"Asians took my arm and my good looks," said Reza. "Still, don't blame them; did the same to several of them. As mentioned, I'm also in a perfect position to sabotage the ship. Then again, maybe I only say that to appear trustworthy, eh?"

"We are not getting anywhere like this," said Sophia. "Everyone, resume your normal duties. From now on, we sleep in shifts. Two people must always be awake until we figure out what is happening."

A memory bubbled up from her subconsciousness. "That reminds me… Something behind the flames. I couldn't get a clear view. It's like my eyes slid right over it."

Reza leaned forward. "Something… indescribable?"

Sophia nodded. "Could be. Valeria, slow the ship. Reza, perform a full scan of the surroundings."

Valeria saluted. Reza jumped to his feet and climbed the ladder to the lab above.

"I think you're right," he said when Sophia joined him at the scanner shortly afterward. "There is an area nearby where the instruments go crazy. They change between showing nothing at all and every possible measurement simultaneously.

Unless there has been more sabotage, this could be it."

"We can't wait until we have found the saboteur. Send out the probe."

"Aye, captain."

***

Reza carried the cylindrical probe in asbestos gloves from the airlock to the lab, put it down on the largest table, and took a deep breath. Everyone was gathered in the lab. Neferu was setting up her easel.

"Put on your protective glasses," said Reza. "We don't know what kind of radiation this could produce."

A small hatch in the side of the probe slid open with a pneumatic hiss; Reza reached inside with a large tong and retrieved a small glass vial.

There was no mistaking the content; it was like seeing nothing and everything all at once; the mind raced to replace boundless potentiality with infinite actualities. Sophia steadied herself against the wall; Neferu dropped her brush on the floor.

Apeiron. The hypothesized proto matter from which everything else had formed at the dawn of the world. Unbounded, infinite, eternal. No longer a mere hypothesis.

Reza lowered the vial back into the probe and shut the hatch. The room returned to normal solidity. "We've got it," he said.

Neferu picked up her brush from the floor. "I'm going to need another look," she said.

"When will you be ready to start the experiments?" said Sophia.

Reza carried the probe to a cabinet by the wall, placed it on a shelf, and locked the fortified glass doors. "We should wait until the saboteur has been found. The experiments must be performed with the utmost care. If current scientific theories are correct, the slightest disturbance could destroy the ship."

***

Sophia spent the rest of the day interviewing the crew, meticulously noting down their daily routine and actions in the days since launch, hoping that the saboteur would give something away. As she studied her notes at the end of the day, an idea came to her.

She switched on the comm system. "Reza. Neferu. Please join us in the control room."

***

Sophia sat in the captain's chair in the circular control room. Valeria reclined in her chair near the instruments on the wall, idly inspecting the panels from the corner of her eye. Neferu sat cross-legged on the carpeted floor. Reza leaned against the wall with his arms crossed.

Sophia rose from her chair and leaned against the armrest, inspecting the room. "As you may have noticed, I have spent the day interviewing you all and charting your actions since launch. This has allowed me to form a full picture of the happenings on the ship. While I could not count on all of you telling the truth, I counted on the fact that cross-referencing all our stories would make any lie stand out from the whole."

"When I compared the different stories, one thing became clear to me…" She paused dramatically.

"That's enough," said Valeria. She stood on the floor, holding a knife in her raised right hand. "One more word, and

I'll put this knife in your lovely neck."

Sophia froze in place like a statue. For a moment, all four people formed a dramatic tableau, like a still from a suspense movie.

Reza was the first to break the silence. "I should have known it was you."

She sneered at him. "Really? I thought my cover was pretty good."

He slowly raised his mechanical arm, pointing right at her. "Precisely. You are too obviously not a spy to not be the spy. Always going on about how you fought the Asians, they killed so many of your friends, blablabla."

"Too bad you didn't figure it out sooner, then. The people who killed my friends are the ones who used them as cannon fodder on the battlefield. I don't blame the Asians. I blame both of our governments. Neither side should have this power for themselves." She turned back to Sophia. "Here is what happens next. You are going to turn this ship around and return to Earth. I'll use one of the emergency chutes to bail out before we land."

"That's not going to happen," said Reza, still pointing at her.

"What are you going to do about it, old man? Rush me from across the room?"

A high-pitched whine emerged from Reza's general location, and a shimmering wave shot from the palm of his mechanical arm. Valeria barely had time to change the expression on her face before the wave struck her in the solar plexus. She collapsed in a pile on the carpet as if someone had turned off a switch; the knife fell from her hands.

Sophia's hair rose on her head, and her skin tingled. The air smelled of ozone. "What the hell was that? There are no weapons allowed on my ship!"

Reza retrieved a small card from his pocket and brandished it in her direction. "Calm down, Captain. I am a duly appointed agent of the ecclesia, charged with ensuring the security of this mission."

Sophia inspected the card and threw it on the floor. "Why was I not informed of this? This is my ship, dammit! I need to know what's going on."

"Don't be silly," said Reza. "Agents always operate incognito until the time is right to reveal ourselves. You should be grateful I was here to fix this mess."

"Fine," said Sophia. "Cuff her to her bed. I want to talk to her when she wakes up."

***

Valeria blinked, groaned, and looked at Reza and Sophia, who sat at the edge of her bed. She pulled the cuffs a few times, and they jangled against the side. Neferu painted the scene from the other side. "This is so great," she said. "The story told by these paintings will outlive the Illiad."

Valeria ran her free hand through her hair and sighed. "I gotta admit I did not see that coming. She caught Sophia's eyes with a penetrating glare. "I'm impressed by your detective work, Captain. I didn't think you would figure things out so quickly."

"Oh, I had no idea it was you," said Sophia. "All of you gave me page after page of boring daily routines. I thought if I pretended to have everything figured out, the saboteur might get nervous and expose themselves."

"What? You didn't notice that my testimony had me doing work in the attic at a time when Neferu claimed she was there alone?"

Sophia produced a stack of papers and leafed through them, dropping several pages haphazardly on the floor. "Oh, right! Here it is. I was so bored that I didn't notice. Too bad no one thought to put a master detective on a Moon mission. Anyway, my plan worked beyond my wildest expectations. I figured the saboteur might get nervous and give me something to work with, not expose themselves completely."

"So, what happens, now?" asked Valeria. "You gonna keep me chained to the bed for the rest of the mission?"

"Pretty much. I will let you walk around and assist with minor tasks, under strict supervision. I'll have to handle all the piloting by myself. It will be awkward but doable. You will watch us complete the mission you tried to destroy."

"We'll see about that," said Valeria, a faint smile on her face. "I only need to get lucky once."

***

Sophia woke from a restless dream in which she chased a spy through a ship that went on forever, climbing a never-ending series of ladders. She checked the chronometer on the side table: The sleep cycle was less than halfway over. Neferu slept soundly on her bunk, but Reza and Valeria were gone. The ladder extended from the ceiling to the floor, and light flowed down from the open hatch like sunlight through a hole in a forest canopy.

She swore, grabbed her uniform, and climbed the ladder.

The lab was empty but fully lit, and the open hatch formed a dark rectangle in the ceiling. She heard sounds of movement from the attic. The probe containing Apeiron watched her from the glass cabinet.

The attic at the top of the ship was dark and filled with a random assortment of equipment and suits. By the airlock, Reza was securing the door. Through the window in the massive airlock door, Valeria looked out. She noticed Sophia and gave her a small wave. Reza followed her gaze and turned.

"Reza! What the hell are you doing?"

"I didn't expect you to wake up so soon," said Reza. "You must have one hell of a metabolism. This is for the greater good. She can't be allowed to jeopardize the mission."

"Let her out! That's an order."

He did not move. "As I said, the ecclesia put me in charge of mission security."

Valeria's muffled voice penetrated the glass: "You should be grateful that he has more guts than you. Let's end this."

Reza pushed a button, a red lamp lit above the door, and the pneumatic sound of moving pistons filled the room. Sophia ran to the door in time to see Valeria flip her the bird. White flames swallowed the offending hand, and for a moment, a ghostly after-image of the middle finger floated in the center of Sophia's vision.

The outer airlock closed again, the flames disappeared, and pitch blackness descended upon the room. The only sensory impression remaining was the steady breathing of Reza close by her side.

"I'll see to it you are punished for this," said Sophia.

"You can try," said Reza. "Let's complete the mission first, shall we?"

**

"Goddammit," said Reza, pounding his unenhanced hand on the burnished lab table. A petri dish of Apeiron jumped half an inch into the air, and its contents flowed like quicksilver, forming tendrils and lakes of potential. Sophia couldn't tell if it reflected light or shone by itself.

"Don't paint that," Reza sneered.

"Don't worry," said Neferu from her easel by the wall. "I'm not that fast."

Reza collapsed into a fold-out chair. "No matter what I do, this stuff refuses to do anything except flow around. What's the point of boundless potential if you can't make anything actual?"

"You are one person," said Sophia. "We'll bring it back to Athens, and the scientists at the Academy will figure it out."

Reza looked at the slowly moving silvery substance in the petri dish. "It's hypnotic to look at, but what does that benefit the state? I was hoping to bring at least some useful data back with us."

Neferu yawned. "This scene would make for a terrible painting. Do something picturesque!"

Reza glowered in her direction but said nothing. He strode to the hatch in the floor and disappeared without a word.

The Apeiron formed strange, undulating patterns in the petri dish. Whenever Sophia tried to look at it, her eyes slid across it to focus on nearby items instead.

Neferu was painting a close-up of the petri dish, using reflective silvern paint.

"You can see that stuff clearly?" asked Sophia.

"Sure. You need to look at it without focusing, like one of those pictures that form a three dee image when you cross your eyes."

"Huh. I guess bringing an artist has practical uses after all." Sophia smiled.

Neferu tilted her head and looked at the dish. "It looks like a little octopus, doesn't it? Woah!"

Sophia followed her gaze and gasped. The Apeiron hung in the air several inches above the petri dish. She blinked and could make out eight silver tentacles extending from a central mass, lazily waving in the air."

"Now it looks even more like an octopus!" said Neferu.

Suction cups formed on the tentacles. Eyes opened on the central mass. The creature now hovered nearly a yard above the dish. Sophia's eyes watered from the effort of trying to stay focused on the creature. "It's reacting to your comments! Try to describe it as something else."

"Uh, Ibis!"

The mass assumed a birdish shape. Weird patterns adorned the wings, but Sophia could not make out any details.

"Maybe you need to be more specific? Let me try. Uh, watermelon!"

The birdlike shape wobbled in the air but did not change.

"Papyrus plant!" said Neferu.

The shape extended, forming a long reed-like stem, nearly touching the ground. Thin sprays of foliage grew from the top.

Reza poked his head up through the hatch. "What the hell are you two doing up here?"

His eyes grew wide, and he jumped onto the lab floor. "What happened? How did you make it do that?"

"It's reacting to Neferu's suggestions," said Sophia.

The Apeiron collapsed back into the petri dish, forming a shimmering puddle.

"Dammit!" said Reza. "I wanted to get some measurements."

"Sorry," said Neferu. "You startled me."

Reza fixed her with his gaze. "That implies it was reacting to your thoughts, not your statements. Try to think of something."

Neferu laughed. "Never tell an artist to 'think of something'. Creativity needs constraints."

Sophie looked at the puddle in the dish. "Strange, how it takes up so much less space now."

"It's unbounded," said Reza. "That's what makes it so valuable. If we could unlock its secrets, we could potentially create anything from the smallest amount. Try to think of a pebble."

Neferu furrowed her brows. In the dish, the shimmer contracted into a tiny ball, rolling gently from side to side.

Reza leaned forward, studying the ball. "Someone could smuggle this thing inside of a ballpoint pen... Now think of a fire."

"What?"

"Don't play stupid. Do it!"

The ball rose into the hair and unfolded into silver flames, a ball of fire hanging in the center of the lab, throwing flickering light onto the walls.

Sophia felt the heat on her face. "Perhaps this is how it began," she said. "Someone wanted light, and there it was."

"That's more of a bonfire than an explosion," said Reza. "But it's a start. Note the heat; it's not only the shape that is malleable. If we can unlock its full potential, the sky's the limit. We could wipe the entire Asian continent off the map with a thimble-full of this stuff!"

The fire abruptly ceased, and a small amorphous blob fell into the dish.

"What!" said Neferu.

"This is a scientific expedition," said Sophia. "Our results should benefit humanity!"

"Europan supremacy will benefit humanity!" said Reza.

"How are we supposed to make any progress with the Asians at our doorstep, forcing us to focus our resources on defending our way of life? Only once our enemies have been neutralized will there be peace and prosperity. You didn't seriously think we would share this stuff with them, did you?"

Neferu waved her paintbrush in his face. "Well, you're not getting my help! I'm a creator, not a destroyer. If you need me for anything else, I'll be downstairs."

She wrapped the canvas, folded the easel, and climbed down the ladder.

An hour later, Reza still stared at the blob in the petri dish. He had shouted himself hoarse, trying out different words as if increasing the volume would cause a more significant response. The Apeiron had been utterly unmoved.

"I guess you need an artist after all," said Sophia, sitting on a chair by the wall. She had no intention of helping Reza but felt it was a good idea to keep an eye on him.

"Art is two steps removed from reality," said Reza with a voice like sandpaper. "Science alone sees Being as it truly is. We will figure this out."

Sophia yawned. "It's getting late. How about we call it a day?"

Reza ignored her.

Neferu already slept soundly on her bunk in the darkened room; no doubt lost in the realms of her imagination. Sophia envied her. She collapsed onto her bunk and curled up under her blanket. The subdued sound of Reza's swearing from above lulled her to sleep like white noise.

***

The louder sound of Reza swearing nearby woke her. "Get

up," he said. "The state needs your patriotic services."

"Let go of me, your big oaf," said Neferu.

His biomechanical arm had grabbed hold of her right shoulder and was pulling her to her feet. "We cannot afford to waste any more time. You'll show me how it's done, and then you can go back to sleep."

Sophia jumped from her bunk. "Stop it, this instant! That's an order."

Reza looked at her unimpressed but did not let go. "As I said, I'm in charge of security on the ship. This is a matter of national security."

"By that argument, you can take charge of anything!"

"Indeed."

He dragged Neferu towards the ladder and pushed her up the steps through the open hatch above. Sophia followed close behind them.

Reza put Neferu down next to the lab table and relinquished his grip. Neferu rubbed her shoulder and winced. "Let's get to work," he said.

"This is mutiny, Reza," said Sophia. "I will have you in front of the magistrate when we return."

"I'll take my chances."

A larger dish containing a larger sample of Apeiron rested on the table.

"I've been poking at this all night," said Reza. "Make it do something."

"Like what?" said Neferu. "Be specific!"

"You did plenty of artsy stuff yesterday. Try to make a weapon."

Neferu rolled her eyes. "Infinite, unbounded potential and you want weapons. Fine."

The sample wobbled and rose from the disk, spinning

around and extending along the vertical axis until it formed a stately longsword with a curvy handguard. The blade of the sword seemed the catch the sun, although the light in the lab was uniform.

Reza scratched his facial scars. "A bit primitive. I was thinking more along the line of… Ow!"

The longsword had toppled and hit him on the head with the blunt side of the blade, a sound like a shovel hitting a rock.

"That felt surprisingly solid… Ow! Stop it, you bitch!"

"You want weapons!" cried Neferu. "This is what weapons feel like, asshole!"

BONK

Reza's mechanical arm struck the Apeiron sword, shattering it into hundreds of tiny droplets flying and bouncing off the walls. Little balls of nothing and everything cutting paths through the air.

Reza stumbled against the lab table, swatting away droplets with his natural arm. "Look what you have done! Control it!"

"Behold, my weapon!" said Neferu. "The explodo-sword! I'm done here."

She strode towards the hatch. "Where do you think you are going?" said Reza, taking a step forward and grabbing for Neferu with his metal arm.

Several droplets struck him in the face; he cried out, lost his footing, and stumbled into Neferu. "Look out!" she yelled, and they both went through the hatch together. A sickening crash below.

Sophia ran to the hatch. Reza lay on top of Neferu on the floor below. He rolled over and assumed a sitting position. Sophia slid down the ladder, jumped off at the last second, and landed next to Neferu. She wasn't moving.

"I'm sorry, I…" said Reza.

Sophia wanted to scream, but no sound would come.

***

Neferu lay on her back in the airlock, hands folded on her chest and her eyes closed. Her nose was broken, but they had managed to cover the rest of the damage, working together in silence. She was supposed to look like she was sleeping, but she didn't.

"This is the only way," said Reza. "We don't have the facilities to store a body for any significant period."

Sophia had not said a word since Neferu had died on her bunk, her final act being to squeeze Sophia's hand.

"I don't like the way she looks," said Sophia. "The folded hands are way too cliché. She wouldn't have liked that. Put them by her side."

Reza shrugged but did as she said. "Is that bet.. Hey!"

Sophia pushed the airlock door with all her strength, and it shut with a metallic bang that reverberated through her bones and into her feet. She turned the handle to secure the lock.

Reza's face at the window. "OPEN THE DOOR." His muffled voice. It sounded far away. Everything felt far away. Was this happening? Maybe she would wake up soon, and Neferu would still be alive. "WHAT ARE YOU DOING!" The sound of his enhanced arm slamming against the inside of the door.

"YOU KNOW THE PENALTY FOR MUTINY!" she shouted at the door. "I'LL TAKE MY CHANCES WITH THE MAGISTRATE."

She pushed the button and watched the Moon consume them both.

She did not wake up, and Neferu remained dead.

She collapsed on her bunk and fell into a dreamless sleep.

She woke in an empty room with only the hum of the cooling system for company.

An alarm was going off in the control room. She slid down the ladder without much urgency and inspected the instruments. The ship was approaching the other end of the tube; the sensors could now detect the rough bark-like surface that contained the lunar flames. She adjusted the scanners, and there it was: A round hole in the bark, roughly the same size as the one they had entered; another moon, invisible from Earth.

Would the other moon have another earth, she wondered, or would there only be darkness? She was not supposed to find out. They had found the Apeiron and explored the interior of the tube. Her objective now was to return to the earth with the spoils; someone else could continue the exploration of the cosmos later.

She did not much care; she adjusted the ship's course, heading straight for the nega-moon, as she decided to call it. Whatever was on the other side could not be worse than the world she came from. She slumped in the captain's chair, a queen with no subjects, sighing with relief at her decision.

The ship passed through the hole, and the viewscreens and sensors showed darkness ahead; the black void swallowed the light of the nega-moon from behind her. Only the solar ring remained, the edge of the known universe, the sun itself still hidden behind the Earth.

Past the solar ring, there was nothing but more darkness—no more rings. If anything was left to discover, it was beyond sensor range and provided no measurable radiation.

The lesson of Columbus remained true, even here; there was no new world to welcome her.

***

Drops of Apeiron still drifted through the lab, bouncing from the walls, floor, and ceiling, showing no signs of losing momentum. She slumped against the wall, exhaled, and watched the drifting droplets forming patterns in the air. As her eyes filled with tears, blurring her vision, she finally saw them clearly. The laboratory and everything in it receded into the blurry background, and the droplets came into focus, spheres of pure potential hovering in front of her.

With a single thought, she caused them all to collapse into a ball the size of a melon. Through the surface, she saw possibility and hope. She remembered Reza's words: A thimble-full could wipe out a continent. Could it create a continent as well?

"Come," she said to the ball hovering in the lab. To her surprise, it worked. As she walked to the ladder and climbed into the attic, the ball hovered behind her.

The window at the outer airlock door showed only blackness, like a square of obsidian set into the metal. Was it even transparent?

A hissing sound as the airlock depressurized. She could hear her breathing inside the suit. She pushed the button on the wall, and the outer airlock door swung open, revealing inky blackness outside. She stepped out, grabbing the side of the ship with the suction gloves.

The ball floated past her, glowing in the dark like a luminescent jellyfish, the light reflecting from the ship's surface. She let her eyes go out of focus, and as the ship turned into a metallic blur at the edge of her vision, the ball became a glowing hole in the void, through which indefinable shapes and colors moved.

Time to see how big this thing could get. The ball started to grow, losing its spherical shape, becoming an amorphous tear in the black velvet of the void.

Would it be possible to create an entire new world? One in which humanity would not be confined to the top of a tiny cylinder; in which new worlds could be discovered; in which there would be plenty of resources for everyone; no reason for endless conflict.

The ball split into a multitude of smaller pieces, forming cylinders, spheres, wheels, and shapes of every other conceivable type, moving among each other in an intricate dance.

What to make first? When creating a new world, where does one start?

She inspected the boundless night.

"Light."

TENEBROUS PILGRIMAGE

Riding the shadow past Einstein,
outrunning the light of realization,
reason, knowledge, and pain.
Attain the moon from the Earth
in a single moment of elation.

The Earth, a glittering globe above.
The light of humanity mere pinpricks
on inky continents.
The shadow pours
into the craters, revealing
silvern regolith.

POLIS CUM LAUDE

The city grows like moss on the forest floor.

I watch from a nearby branch,

As roads form grids of rivulets.

As exuberant life settles into steady rhythms.

Are they happier? I trill,

As they construct the frames of their days.

The moss covers the trunks of former trees.

Does the new green compare to the leaves?

Moss and trees both belong to the woods.

BLURB

"We choose to go THROUGH the moon!"

In a world in which the Greek philosopher Anaximander was right about everything, Sophia Aetós has lived her life on top of the flat cylinder of the Earth as the nations of Europa, Asia, and Libya fight for control over meager territory.

Now, she must lead the first Europan expedition into the moon, which, as every child knows, is a circular hole in a massive ring of bark filled with pale fire. The goal of the expedition: To locate Apeiron, the mythical ur-substance from which all other matter derives.

It soon becomes clear that not everyone wants the mission to succeed. At least one crew member is a saboteur, willing to sacrifice their life to see the ship consumed by Moon fire.

Not only that but factions in the Europan government wish to use Apeiron for military purposes, potentially launching an all-consuming world war. Their agents, too, have infiltrated the team.

Sofia must draw on both her leadership abilities and scientific skills in a desperate bid to save the expedition and ensure that it will save the world, not destroy it.

ABOUT THE AUTHOR

Simon Christiansen is a writer, poet, and game designer living in Denmark. His stories have been published in a variety of literary journals, and he has written award-winning works of interactive fiction. He is the recipient of three Xyzzy awards for interactive fiction and has been shortlisted for the Niels Klim award for best Danish science fiction novelette.

When not writing, he enjoys reading, juggling, and walking. Visit his website at www.sichris.com.

Made in the USA
Columbia, SC
08 October 2023